Produced by Kroha Associates, Inc.
Middletown, Connecticut.

Printed in the United States of America.

ISBN 1-56326-110-3

Puppies
Are Coming

By Ruth Lerner Perle

One day Minnie came running over to her friends in the playground. "Guess what! Fifi is going to have puppies!" she cried.

"That's great!" Clarabelle said. "Could I adopt one?"

"I'd like one, too," Lilly said. "I could give a puppy a good home."

"I don't know how many puppies Fifi will have, but we'll know soon enough. The veterinarian thinks she'll have them in about two weeks," Minnie said.

The girls went home with Minnie and took turns petting Fifi and scratching her behind her ears.

"Fifi's basket looks old and ragged," Minnie said. "She should have a nice new place to have her puppies."

Minnie and her friends spent the rest of the week getting ready for the happy event.

Lilly brought
a big new basket.

Daisy and Clarabelle brought cozy blankets.

And Penny brought a soft pillow with a little ruffle around the edge.

They spent a whole afternoon painting the basket and decorating it with pretty designs.

Fifi watched as Minnie placed the new basket in the corner of the playroom.

"There you are, Fifi," Minnie said. "Now you have a nice new place to rest and wait for your babies. I sure hope you'll have them soon!"

"You won't need this old basket now that you have a special new one," Minnie said. She picked up Fifi's old bed and took it up to the attic.

Now that Fifi's basket was ready, there was nothing to do but wait. So, day after day, the girls came to Minnie's house and did just that. They waited and waited and waited.

Time seemed to pass more and more slowly, and Minnie was getting anxious.

Where are those puppies? Minnie thought. *Maybe I'm doing something wrong. Maybe I should be doing something special for Fifi.*

The next day, the girls decided to go to the library to look for a book about dogs. Minnie found a book that had a chapter about newborn puppies and their mothers. She took the book off the shelf and sat down to read it. When Minnie was done, Penny asked, "Well, why haven't the puppies come?"

"What have we done wrong?" Clarabelle wanted to know.

"What should we be doing?" asked Daisy.

Minnie laughed. "What we're doing wrong is trying too hard to do things right. The best thing we can do for Fifi is to leave her alone."

The next day, the girls gathered at Minnie's house.

"I have an idea!" Lilly said. "It's a beautiful day. We haven't been to the park in two weeks. Let's go out and have some fun. That will take our minds off waiting for those puppies."

Everyone agreed and off they went.

The girls went to the playground. They played hopscotch, they jumped rope, and they went on the swings and the seesaw.

"Oh, this is fun!" Daisy shouted. "I've missed playing in the park."

After they left the playground, the girls walked around the lake. As they passed the boathouse, Clarabelle's face suddenly lit up.

"Let's go rowing!" she suggested.

Within minutes the girls had rented a bright red boat and were rowing across the lake. Then they pulled up the oars and floated lazily in the water.

"I was just thinking about Fifi," Minnie said. "I wonder how many puppies she'll have."

"I wonder what they'll look like," said Penny.

"What shall we name them?" Lilly asked.

After a while, Minnie noticed that it was getting dark. She looked at her watch.

"Oh, dear! We've been out here more than an hour!" she cried. "The time went by so fast! We'd better hurry back home and check on Fifi." The girls rowed back quickly and then ran all the way to Minnie's house.

"Fifi! Fifi!" Minnie called as she opened the front door, but there was no answer.

Now Minnie was really worried. Fifi wasn't barking or coming to greet her.

The girls ran to the playroom and looked in the pretty basket they had prepared, but it was empty.

"Where can Fifi be?" Daisy cried. "Maybe we shouldn't have left her alone after all!"

The girls looked under the stairs, in the closets, and in the yard.

"Fifi! Fifi!" they called. But there was no sound.

Just then, Minnie thought she heard a little bark coming from the attic. Holding her breath, Minnie raced up the steps and turned on the light. There, curled up inside her old ragged basket, was Fifi!

"Fifi? What are you doing here?" Minnie whispered. She stepped closer to get a better look. Then she saw the furry little puppies that were snuggled up next to Fifi.

Minnie motioned to her friends to be quiet, and they tiptoed over to look at the new mother and her puppies.

"They're here at last!" Minnie whispered. "We planned to have a special basket for Fifi, but I guess she had plans of her own."

Minnie bent down closer to Fifi. "Thank goodness you're safe and our waiting is over," she said softly.

Fifi wagged her tail as if to say, *Some things just can't be rushed!*

Fifi was a wonderful mother! And those fluffy puppies were sure worth waiting for!